Previously published in Switzerland
under the title *Das schönste Lied*

Illustrations Copyright © 1980 by bohem press, Zürich, Switzerland

Text Copyright © 1977 by Verlag Ernst Kaufmann, Lahr, Germany

ISBN 0-316-10117-6

Library of Congress Catalog Card No. 81-80858

First American Edition

The Most Beautiful Song

by Max Bolliger

Illustrations by Jindra Čapek

Little, Brown and Company

Boston

Once upon a time a king had a dream.

In his dream he saw a tree, and on that tree sat a bird
singing the most beautiful song the king had ever heard.

The next morning the king called the birdcatcher from
where the youth sat playing his flute. The king told him:
"I had a dream. I saw a tree, and on that tree sat a bird
singing the most beautiful song I ever heard. I must hear
that song again. Go and catch the bird for me."

"Yes, sire," said the birdcatcher. "But please, sire, can you tell me what kind of bird it was?" But the king didn't know. "Just go and catch it," he thundered. "I give you seven days."

The birdcatcher was afraid of the king's anger, so he took his flute and his net and went into the garden. He hid behind a wall and played the joyful song of the blackbird. When the blackbird left its nest and flew toward the music, he caught it and brought it to the king. The king listened to the blackbird's song.

"No," said the king. "That's not the most beautiful song."

On the second day the birdcatcher took his flute and
his net and went into the fields. He hid behind a hedge
and played the sweet song of the lark. When the lark
left its nest, he caught it with the net, put it into a
cage, and brought it to the king.

"No," said the king. "That is not the right song."

The birdcatcher gave a sigh, but he took his flute and
his net and went to the stream. He hid behind a stone
and played the song of the golden oriole, and when he
had caught.the beautiful bird, he put it into a cage and
brought it to the king.

The king frowned when he heard the oriole sing.
"No," said the king, "that is still not the right one."

On the fourth day the birdcatcher took his flute and
his net and went into the woods. He hid behind a tree
and played the pure song of the thrush. When the thrush
left its nest, he caught it with a net, put it into a cage,
and brought it to the king.

"No, no," roared the king. "That is still not the most
beautiful song. You are a poor birdcatcher indeed.
Go and find me the bird I heard in my dream."

The birdcatcher trembled in fear of the king, but on the fifth day he took his flute and his net and went to the edge of the forest. He hid behind a bush and played the song of the wren. And when the wren flew into the air, he caught it, put it into a cage, and brought it to the king.

"No," said the king. "That's not the right one. If you cannot bring me the bird with the most beautiful song soon, you will be thrown into prison."

On the sixth day the birdcatcher took his flute and his net and went into the park. He hid behind a fountain and played the silvery song of the nightingale. When the nightingale left its nest, he caught it with a net, put it into a cage, and brought it to the king.

When the king heard the nightingale sing, he flew
into a rage. "No, that is not the one. I give you one
more day. Bring the bird with the most beautiful song
tomorrow, or you will be sorry."

The birdcatcher didn't know any more bird songs to play, so on the seventh day he went to the castle with a heavy heart. He did not try to hide, but he took out his flute and played his own song. "This is the last time I will play my own song," he thought, "because now the king will throw me into prison and take away my flute."

He played his song more beautifully than he had ever done before. The king, who was having breakfast, put down his knife and fork. "That's it!" he cried. "The song I heard in my dream. The most beautiful song."

He commanded that the birdcatcher be brought
before him at once.
"Where is the bird?" he asked.

"It was not a bird," said the birdcatcher. "It was my own song."

The king was amazed. To show his pleasure, he called
for a celebration.

The birds that the birdcatcher had caged were set free,
and the birdcatcher too was given his freedom. He went
on his way, promising to return once a year so that the
king once again could hear the most beautiful song.